For Kerry, Rebecca, and Heather,
my fairy friends forever
—S. F.

For Mom and Dad,
with all my love
—C. K.

Henry Holt and Company, LLC
Publishers since 1866
175 Fifth Avenue, New York, New York 10010
mackids.com

Library of Congress Cataloging-in-Publication Data is available.
Fliess, Sue.
A fairy friend / Sue Fliess ; illustrated by Claire Keane. — First edition.
pages cm
Summary: Fairies are all around us, and if you want to have one come to you, build a fairy house to have a fairy visit.
ISBN 978-1-62779-081-9 (hardback)
[1. Stories in rhyme. 2. Fairies—Fiction. 3. Magic—Fiction.] I. Keane, Claire, illustrator. II. Title.
PZ8.3.F642Fai 2016   [E]—dc23   2015015547

Our books may be purchased in bulk for promotional, educational, or business use.
Please contact your local bookseller or the Macmillan Corporate and Premium Sales Department at
(800) 221-7945 ext. 5442 or by e-mail at MacmillanSpecialMarkets@macmillan.com.

First Edition—2016 / Typography hand-lettered by Claire Keane
The illustrations for this book were painted in watercolor and Photoshop.
Printed in China by RR Donnelley Asia Printing Solutions Ltd., Dongguan City, Guangdong Province

1 3 5 7 9 10 8 6 4 2

A FAIRY FRIEND

WRITTEN BY SUE FLIESS
ILLUSTRATED BY CLAIRE KEANE

Christy Ottaviano Books
Henry Holt and Company
New York

There are fairies in the sky.
All around you, fairies fly,
Flit and flutter, tumble, twirl,
When the wind blows, fairies swirl . . .

Skip through flowers,

Zip through trees,

Hum and buzz among the bees.

Friendly fairies soar the skies,
Ride the backs of dragonflies.

Wings of fairies shimmer, spark,
Twinkle, glimmer in the dark.

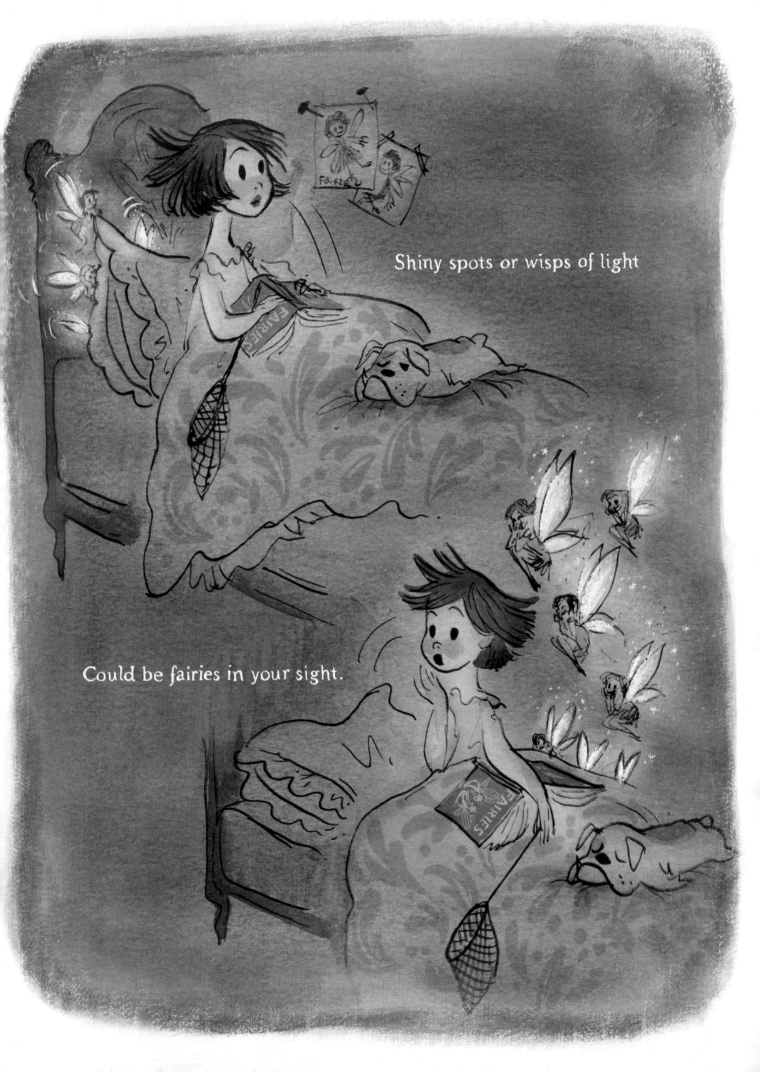

Shiny spots or wisps of light

Could be fairies in your sight.

If you want a fairy friend,
One who'll be there till the end . . .

You must know just where to look—

Search in every niche and nook.

Want to have one come to you?
Here is what you'll need to do . . .

Build a house of twigs and blooms,
Decorate her fairy rooms—

Walls of blossoms, cotton floor,
Sparrow feather for her door.

Mossy rooftop, pebble path,
Mushroom cap to take her bath.
Thistle fluff for fairy's bed,
Willow fuzz to rest her head.

Make for her a fairy swing:
Tie a nutshell to a string.

Cook a flower-petal stew.

Serve it, and she'll come to you.

Very slowly tiptoe near.
Quiet, or she'll disappear.

Gently offer out your hand. . . .
Name your fairy and she'll land.
While she's resting in your palm,
Whisper softly, keep her calm . .

She will teach you how to fly,
Sail with you through forest sky,

Shower you with fairy charm,

Keep you safe from hurt and harm.

Forever friends you two will be,
Fairykin and fancy-free.

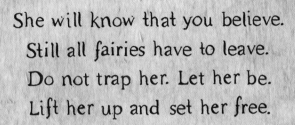

She will know that you believe.
Still all fairies have to leave.
Do not trap her. Let her be.
Lift her up and set her free.

Time may pass while she's away,
But do not let your heart dismay.
For if you're thoughtful, kind, and true,
Your fairy will return to you!